Ten Timid Ghosts

For
Bethany
and Brendan

Library of Congress Cataloging-in-Publication Data
O'Connell, Jennifer.
    Ten timid ghosts / by Jennifer O'Connell.
       p. cm.
    Summary: A witch tries to scare ten ghosts out of the haunted house where they live,
but in the end, they play a trick on her.
    ISBN-13: 978-0-439-15804-8 (pbk.)
    ISBN-10: 0-439-15804-4
    [1. Witches—Fiction. 2. Ghosts—Fiction. 3. Haunted Houses—Fiction. 4. Counting.]
I. Title.
PZ7.0216 Te 2000
[E]-dc21   99-046427

12 11 10 9 8 7 6 5 4 3 2 1   7 8 9 10 11 12/0

Printed in the U.S.A.
First printing, September 2000

23

Ten Timid Ghosts

by Jennifer O'Connell

Cartwheel
·B·O·O·K·S·®

SCHOLASTIC INC.

New York Toronto London Auckland Sydney
Mexico City New Delhi Hong Kong Buenos Aires

10

Ten timid ghosts in a haunted house –
A witch moved in and wanted them out.

One saw a skeleton
and let out a whine.
He flew to the woods
and then there were nine.

Nine timid ghosts in a haunted house –
A witch moved in and wanted them out.
One saw a bat
and didn't wait.
She flew to the woods
and then there were eight.

Eight timid ghosts in a haunted house ~
A witch moved in and wanted them out.
One saw a ghoul
and screamed, "Oh, my heaven!"
He flew to the woods
and then there were seven.

Seven timid ghosts in a haunted house ~
A witch moved in and wanted them out.
One saw a cat.
What a terrible fix!
She flew to the woods
and then there were six.

Six timid ghosts in a haunted house -
A witch moved in and wanted them out.
One saw an owl
and took a dive.
He flew to the woods
and then there were five.

Five timid ghosts in a haunted house –
A witch moved in and wanted them
One saw a vampire
and dashed to the door.
She flew to the woods
and then there were four.

Four timid ghosts in a haunted house –
A witch moved in and wanted them out.
One saw a monster
and was as scared as could be.
He flew to the woods
and then there were three.

3

Three timid ghosts in a haunted house –
A witch moved in and wanted them out.
One saw a spider
and what did she do?
She flew to the woods
and then there were two.

Two timid ghosts in a haunted house~
A witch moved in and wanted them out.
One saw a rat
and started to run.
He flew to the woods
and then there was one.

One clever ghost in a haunted house~
A witch moved in and wanted her out.
    She saw the witch
        coming undone!
            She flew to the woods
                and then there were none.

10 Ten angry ghosts in the deep dark wood ~
"That witch is too tricky and just no good."
"This isn't fair! We live in there!"
"Let's band together and give her a scare!"

One mean old witch in a haunted house —
Ten brave ghosts — WANTED HER OUT. . . .

The witch saw the ghosts
and howled with fear.
She tore out the door screaming,
"GET ME OUT OF HERE!"